W9-AOM-931

BLUEY

SWIM SCHOOL

PENGUIN YOUNG READERS LICENSES
An imprint of Penguin Random House LLC, New York

First published in Australia by Puffin Books, 2023

First published in the United States of America by Penguin Young Readers Licenses,
an imprint of Penguin Random House LLC, New York, 2024

This book is based on the TV series *Bluey*.

Visit us online at penguinrandomhouse.com.

Manufactured in China

ISBN 9780593752791 (pbk)
ISBN 9780593752807 (hc)

10 9 8 7 6 5 4 3 2 1 HH
10 9 8 7 6 5 4 3 2 1 HH

Bluey and her family are on holiday.

"Bingo, it's a bit dangerous to run by the pool," says Dad.

"Sorry," says Bingo and stops.

But then Bluey runs in.

LET'S PLAY SWIM SCHOOL!

"Dad, Bluey's running by the pool!" says Bingo.

"Don't be a dobber," says Dad.

"But Bluey's doing something dangerous," says Bingo, confused. "Shouldn't I dob then?"

Dad doesn't know how to answer that. "Uh . . . Chilli?"

Mum just shrugs.

It's time for Swim School. The students have to pass all the lessons in Little Fish before they can move up to Big Fish.

"Hello, darlings! I'm Karen," says the teacher.

Merifyndor, Sharon, and Bevan are a family in the Little Fish class. Karen is teaching them to kick, when Bevan starts mucking around.

"Bevan isn't doing it properly," dobs Sharon.

DOO-DOO-DOO!

"Is Bevan doing anything **DANGEROUS?**" asks Karen.

"Well, no."

"Then don't be a dobber, sweetie."

The family keeps practicing kicking until Merifyndor disappears underwater . . .

"Karen, Merifyndor just poked me!" dobs Bevan.

HANDS TO YOURSELF, PLEASE, YOUNG LADY!

"Hang on!" says Sharon. "Shouldn't Bevan get in trouble for dobbing, like I did?"

"Yes. Bevan, no dobbing," says Karen.

"Shouldn't **SHARON** get in trouble for dobbing on me about dobbing on Merifyndor?" he asks.

"Oh, yes. Bad Sharon."

Karen has had enough. "Okay, class, there's a new rule. **NO MORE DOBBING!**"

"Unless someone is in danger," says Sharon.

Karen nods. "Remember, you are a **FAMILY**."

"Let's work together!" says Bevan.

When they work together, Merifyndor, Sharon, and Bevan are excellent Little Fish. They learn doggy-paddle, monkeying, and . . . **NINJA KICKS!**

Karen is very proud. "Well done, poppets.
You all get to move up to Big Fish!"

"Good luck," says Karen.

"Wait!" says Sharon. "Aren't you our teacher
for Big Fish?"

"Oh no. Margaret takes
Big Fish," says Karen.
"Goodbye!"

"I have a feeling we're not going to like
Margaret . . . ," says Bevan.

"I'm Margaret. I'm not as **nice** as Karen."

"Don't worry about us. Karen taught us to work as a family and never to dob," says Sharon.

"Well, I **Like** dobbing. If you don't dob, you won't pass."

"But I thought dobbing was bad," says Merifyndor.

"No, dobbing is **GOOD!**"

The family doesn't think much of that.

"We're going to pass Big Fish without dobbing."

But Big Fish is pretty hard.

Margaret sits on you during backstroke . . .

and while you're swimming across the pool.

She even blows on your ears
while you're starfishing!

ANOTHER FAIL!

Sharon calls a
family meeting.

I WANT KAREN BACK.

MARGARET IS A SILLY
OLD WATERMELON HEAD.

"What if we just refuse to do what she says?"
Sharon suggests.

"Yeah!" Bevan agrees. "Let's stick together."

It's a good plan, but before they can try it . . .

Merifyndor dobs them in!

"Excellent dobbing," says Margaret. "You just passed Big Fish."

"Merifyndor!" Bevan shouts. "Did you dob on us?!"

Now everyone starts to dob, and no one gets better at swimming.

"Merifyndor called you a **SILLY OLD WATERMELON HEAD!**"

"But Sharon **PEEKED** in Marco Polo!"

FAIL!

19

Sharon, Margaret, and Merifyndor race to get out of the water.

"You two pass Big Fish," Margaret tells Sharon and Merifyndor. "Bevan, you fail, ya big grub!"

Merifyndor has passed the class,
but something isn't right.

Dobbing on her family doesn't feel very good.

"If Bevan fails, then I want to fail, too," Merifyndor says.

HI-YAH!

She ninja-kicks into the pool.

"I'm with Merifyndor."

"Well, fine," says Margaret. "You all fail."

GOOD ONE, SIS!

But then . . .

SURPRISE!

"Welcome back to Little Fish," says Karen.
"I'm so proud of you all."

"Why is the water warmer here?"

HOW TO DRAW BLUEY!

Follow the lines from each step until you finish drawing Bluey for real life.

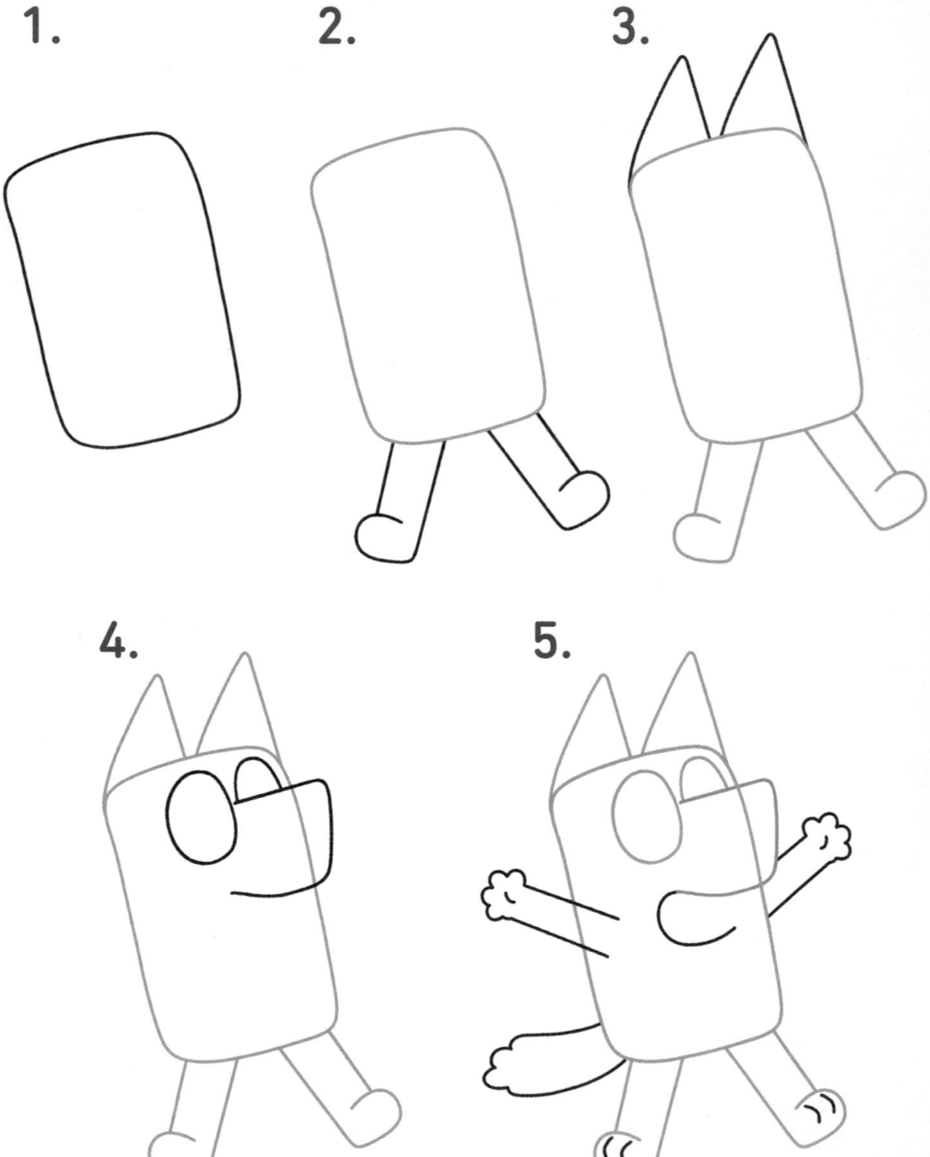

1.

2.

3.

4.

5.

6.

7.

8.

9.

HOW TO DRAW BINGO!

Follow the lines from each step until
you finish drawing Bingo.

1.

2.

3.

4.

5.

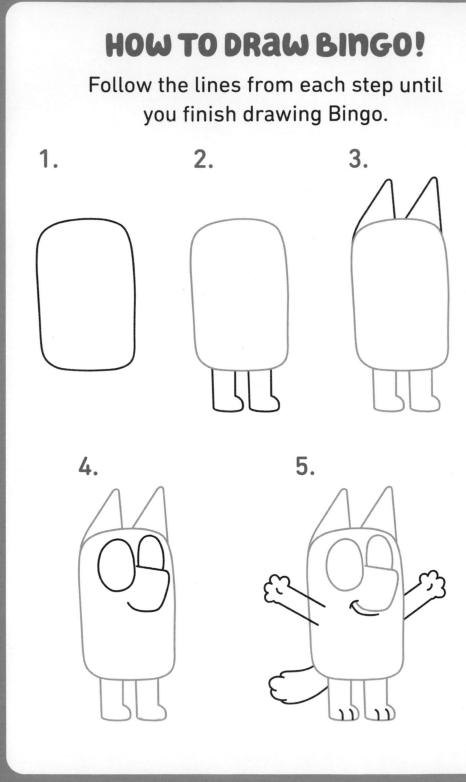

6.

7.

8.

9.

DRAW BLUEY AND BINGO HERE!